When i grow UP

For Caspar – T.M.

For the child in us all – S.A.

When I Grow Up was originally published in the United Kingdom by Scholastic Children's Books in 2017.

ISBN 978-1-338-32566-9

Text copyright © 2017 by Tim Minchin. Illustrations copyright © 2017 by Steve Antony. All rights reserved. Published by Scholastic Inc., *Publishers since 1920.* SCHOLASTIC and associated logos are trademarks and/or registered trademarks of Scholastic Inc.

12 11 10 9 8 7 6 5 4 3 2 1   18 19 20 21 22 23

Printed in the U.S.A.   169

Originally published in hardcover by Scholastic Press, April 2018

First Scholastic paperback printing, September 2018

WHEN

Tim Minchin's
i Grow Up

Illustrated by Steve Antony

SCHOLASTIC INC.

When I grow up, I will be **tall** enough to reach the branches that I have to reach

to climb the trees you get to climb

when you're grown-up.

And when I grow up, I will be **smart** enough to answer all the questions

that you need to know the answers to
before you're grown-up.

And when I grow up, I will

eat sweets every day on the way to work, and I . . .

...will go to bed late every night.

And I will wake up when the sun comes up and I . . .

... will watch cartoons   until my eyes go square, and I won't **care**, 'cause I'll be all grown-up when I grow up.

I will be **strong** enough
to carry all the heavy things
you have to haul around with you
when you're a grown-up.

And
when I grow up,
I will be
brave enough
to fight the
creatures

that
you have
to
fight

beneath

your

bed

each

night

to be a grown-up.

And when I grow up, I will have treats every day . . .

...and I'll **play**
with **things**

that mums pretend that mums
don't think are fun.

And I will **wake up** when the sun comes up and I will spend all day just lying in the sun

and I won't burn 'cause I'll be all grown-up when I grow up.

When I grow up.

When I grow up.

When I grow up.

Tim Minchin is a Tony Award–winning musician, comedian, actor, and writer. In 2009, he was commissioned by the Royal Shakespeare Company to write the music and lyrics for a stage adaptation of Roald Dahl's *Matilda*. *Matilda the Musical* has won over fifty international awards, including seven Olivier Awards and five Tony Awards. Other works include *Dark Side* and *Tim Minchin and the Heritage Orchestra*. Tim also wrote and composed the music for *Groundhog Day: The Musical*. He lives in Sydney, Australia and can be found online at www.timminchin.com.

Steve Antony is the popular author and illustrator of *Please, Mr. Panda*; *I'll Wait, Mr. Panda*; *Thank You, Mr. Panda*; *The Queen's Hat*; *Green Lizards vs. Red Rectangles*; and *Betty Goes Bananas*. *The Queen's Hat* was nominated for the Kate Greenaway Medal in the UK. Steve lives in Swindon, England. Visit him online at www.steveantony.com.